GIRLZRO

Camping Chaos

Shey Kettle

illustrated by
Meredith Thomas

First published in 2006 by
MACMILLAN EDUCATION AUSTRALIA PTY LTD
627 Chapel Street, South Yarra, Australia 3141

This edition first published in the United States of America
in 2006 by MONDO Publishing.

For information contact:
MONDO Publishing
980 Avenue of the Americas
New York, NY 10018

Visit our web site at http://www.mondopub.com

06 07 08 09 10   9 8 7 6 5 4 3 2 1

ISBN 1-59336-937-9 (PB)

Series created by Felice Arena and Phil Kettle
Project Management by Limelight Press Pty Ltd
Cover and text design by Lore Foye
Illustrations by Meredith Thomas

Printed in Hong Kong

GiRLZROCK!

CONTENTS

Mai   Carly

CHAPTER 1

We're Away!

Carly and Mai are going camping during the summer holidays with Carly's mom.

Mai "I'm psyched that your mom asked me to come. It'll be so cool."

Carly "I can't believe Mom thinks four bags are way too many to take camping."

Mai "I don't think mothers realize that great adventurers like us get really dirty and need to change outfits all the time."

Carly "Yeah, but mine will when she has to wash our clothes."

Mai "Do you think there'll be other kids at the campground?"

Carly "I hope so. Last year I met these really cool girls, Jess and Sophie, and we did everything together."

Mai "Maybe they'll be there again."

Carly "That'd be cool. You'd really like them."

Mai "I'm glad we're sharing a tent. Last time I went camping I had to sleep in the same tent as my stinky brother."

Carly "Ahh, gross!"

Mai "Boys always smell really bad... especially brothers."

Carly "And they snore, too."

CHAPTER 2

Tent Spotting

They head off and arrive at the
campground two hours later.

Mai "This place is awesome."
Carly "It sure is. Let's set up our
tent near the water."

Mai "Cool! Then we can sit right out front and fish."

Carly "And I'll catch the biggest fish ever with my new rod."

Mai "You mean the second biggest fish. My rod may be old, but it's been around. It knows how to find the best and biggest fish."

Carly "I wish we didn't bring all these bags. There's hardly any room now for our sleeping bags."

Mai "I know. It didn't look like that much when we were packing."

Carly "Oh, well, if we have to sleep with it all, at least clothes are soft."

Mai "Just don't tell your mom that we brought too much. She'll tell my mom and then they'll think that they're right...again."

Carly "How come they always just know stuff?"

Both girls sigh.

CHAPTER 3

A Juicy Idea

After pitching their tent, Carly and
Mai take a break on the beach.

Mai "So, are we going fishing or
exploring?"
Carly "Both. We can go exploring to
find a great place to fish!"
Mai "Hey, cool!"

Carly "We could paddle out to sea on our boogie boards and look for a whole new place where nobody's ever been...while we fish!"

Mai "Great idea. But what if we hook a huge fish on one of our lines?"

Carly "We might get towed to the other side of the world and never be heard from again."

Mai "As if! But maybe it's not such a good idea to paddle out. We wouldn't want to get stranded. Let's get going. I'll get the bait."

Mai gets a bucket of worms out of the back of the car.

Mai "Look, there are tons of big, juicy worms!"

Carly "Good, fish love worms."

Mai "I wonder why?"

Carly "They must taste good."

Mai "Yeah? So why don't we eat them...barbecued and with lots of ketchup on them?"

Carly (holding a worm) "If you think they're so good, why don't you try one then?"

Mai "No thanks! Worms are gross enough without eating them."

Carly "I think the worst thing about fishing is cleaning the fish. If I catch any, I'm gonna let them go."

Mai "Me, too. The only fish I wanna eat are the ones that are in fish sticks."

CHAPTER 4

Island Girlz

The girls spot a sand bank about forty yards from the shore.

Mai "Look at that sand sticking up above the water. It's like an island."

Carly "Let's wade out there and fish."

The girls collect all they need for their great adventure—fishing rods, a bucket, and the worms. They put on their life jackets and some sunscreen.

Mai "Why are you putting your sneakers on when we're about to walk through water?"

Carly "Haven't you ever heard of
crabs? Well, they have great big
claws...and we have small toes!"

Mai "Right, I get the picture. I think
I'll wear my sneakers, too. I wanna
make sure I keep all my toes!"

Mai and Carly wade through the water toward the sand bank.

Mai "I really do feel like a great explorer."

Carly "So do I. It's like we've just discovered a whole new country. I bet the fish near this island will be huge."

Mai "Yeah, they'll be gigantic 'cause nobody's ever tried to catch them."

The girls step on to the sand.

Carly "I claim this island in the name of Carly and Mai."

Mai "May it be our place forever...or at least for the whole vacation!"

Carly "So, what should we call our island?"

Mai "It needs a really cool name."

Carly "How about Girlz Island?"

Mai "Yeah, that's a great name! Let's write it in the sand."

The girls write "Girlz Island" in large letters in the sand.

Mai "Now anybody that comes near it will know it's ours."

Carly "I know what else we could write in the sand."

Carly writes "No boys allowed."

Mai "I hope that keeps them away. We don't want our island polluted."

Carly "With boy germs! Yuck! Come on, it's time we caught some seriously big fish."

The girls take off their life jackets. Carly pulls a big worm from the bucket and shows it to Mai.

Carly "This'll catch a really big fish."

Carly threads the worm onto the hook.

Mai "Doesn't that hurt the worm?"
Carly "I don't think so. It's probably just like getting your ear pierced."
Mai "But without the ice! Hey, I think our island is starting to shrink."

Carly "What? Maybe the tide's come in but it shouldn't come in any closer. Trust me."

Mai (worriedly) "Okay, Miss Expert. I hope you're right. That water's pretty close to us now."

The girls cast out their lines. Soon Carly gets a bite.

Carly (gripping her rod hard) "I think I've caught the biggest fish in the entire ocean!"

Mai "It must be a whale!"

Carly "Whales aren't fish, they're mammals. Help me, Mai, my arms are about to be pulled off!"

Mai grabs on to Carly's fishing rod and helps her to reel in the fish.

Mai "Maybe it's one of those fish with razor-sharp teeth."

Carly "Yeah, well, whatever it is, it's huge."

Mai "Keep reeling it in, Carly. I'm sure it's getting closer."

CHAPTER 5

Trouble in Paradise

Soon there is a huge fish flapping
around on the sand.

Mai "So, what do we do with it now
that we've caught it?"

Carly "I think we should let it go."

Mai "So do I, but it's gonna be hard to move, and we've got to take out the hook."

Carly "Can you grab its tail?"

Carly and Mai manage to drag the fish back into the water. As they do, the hook drops out of its mouth and the fish swims away.

Mai "Off you go, fishy, back where you belong."

Carly "That was fun, but exhausting! Let's take a rest."

Carly and Mai lie down on the sand and look up at the sky.

Mai "That cloud looks like a car."

Carly "And that one looks like a great fisherman...just like me!"

As the girls stare into the sky, they feel their toes getting wet. Suddenly, they spring to their feet. They can't believe their eyes.

Carly "Oh, no! The tide has come in and our island's almost covered."

Mai "What now, Miss Expert?"

The girls put their life jackets back on and gather up their gear. They wade into the water.

Carly "It's too deep. We could swim but we'll never get all our stuff back. We need someone to help."

Mai "But no one's around, and your mom's gone to make lunch."

Carly "We'll just have to yell. Heeelp! Sommeonnee!"

Just then, the girls spot a man in a small boat off in the distance.

Mai (waving her arms) "Hey, mister, help! We can't get back."
Carly and Mai (shouting) "Heeelp!"

The man looks up and sees the girls. He motors over and picks them up.

Mai "Thanks, mister. That was close! We almost lost all our gear."

Carly "The campsite sure looks
good, and I'm starved. I don't think
Mom'll be too pleased about this,
though. She's always telling me to
keep an eye on the tides."

Mai "Yeah, but we can say we
discovered a brand new island."

Carly (pointing) "Yeah, right, and
that we lost one, too!"

Mai

GIRLZROCK!
Camping
Lingo

Carly

bait What you put on the end of a fishing hook to attract and catch fish.

campground A place where tents can be put up for temporary shelter while camping.

guy-line A rope used to keep the tent steady and to prevent it from blowing away.

pitching Setting up a tent and making sure it's firmly in place.

tent stake A stick that you put in the ground and that the guy-line attaches to.

GIRLZROCK!

Camping Musts

☆ Make sure you don't pitch your tent *too* close to the water's edge. The tide might come in and fill your tent.

☆ Always wear a hat when you are outside during the day to protect your face from the sun.

☆ Make sure you don't leave any food out overnight. You don't want to be visited by bears or other animals while you sleep.

☆ Always take a flashlight to bed with you. There is nothing worse than getting up to go to the bathroom and not being able to find your way through all those creepy woods—eek!

☆ Take plenty of food, especially yummy stuff like marshmallows that you can toast over an open fire.

☆ Before you go to sleep, tell scary ghost stories around the campfire.

☆ Make sure that you put out the campfire before you go to bed.

☆ Bring enough bait so that you can catch plenty of fish.

☆ Always tell an adult if you are going away from the campsite in case you get lost or stranded on an island!

GIRLZROCK!
Camping
Instant Info

🏕 Tents can be very simple or very fancy. The most basic tent is a temporary shelter made from a piece of fabric draped between two poles.

🏕 Tents have been used since the Stone Age. They have protected people from weather and have provided space for gatherings.

🏕 The highest tides on Earth occur in Nova Scotia's Minas Basin in Canada. The tide here can be as high as 52 feet (16 meters)!

The Girl Scouts were formed in 1912 by Juliette "Daisy" Gordon Low. It started with just 18 members but now has around 3.6 million members.

The best tents have mosquito nets and fly screens that protect you from getting bitten by all the creepy-crawlies out there.

To keep animals away from your campsite, spray your garbage with ammonia.

GIRLZ ROCK!
Think Tank

1 Where do Carly and Mai set up their tent?

2 Why does Carly put on her sneakers to walk through the water?

3 What do Carly and Mai call their island?

4 What is one of the yummiest foods to cook over an open fire?

5 What are good things to use as bait?

6 If you went fishing, would you keep the fish you caught or let them go? Explain why.

7 Do you think it was a good idea for Carly and Mai to go fishing without an adult? Why or why not?

8 What do you think will happen to Carly and Mai when they get back to the campground?

Answers

The following answers appear inverted (upside-down) on the page:

1 Carly and Mai set up their tent near the water.

2 Carly puts on her sneakers to protect her toes from crabs in the water.

3 Carly and Mai call their island Girlz Island.

4 Marshmallows are one of the yummiest foods to cook over an open fire.

5 Worms, flies, and pieces of fish are good to use as bait.

6 Answers will vary.

7 Answers will vary.

8 Answers will vary.

How did you score?

- If you got most of the answers correct, you're ready to go camping and sleep in your own tent.

- If you got more than half of the answers correct, then maybe you should sleep in the same tent as your parents for a while.

- If you got less than half of the answers correct, stick to staying in motels when you go away.

Hey, Girls!

I hope that you have as much fun reading my story as I have had writing it. I loved reading and writing stories when I was young.

At school, why don't you use "Camping Chaos" as a play, and you and your friends can be the actors.

Bring in some fishing gear from home. Use sheets for the tents. Maybe you could have your play outside and make a campfire.

So...have you decided who is going to be Mai and who is going to be Carly? Now, with your friends, read and act out this play in front of your classmates. It'll definitely make the whole class laugh.

You can also take the story home and get someone to act out the parts with you.

So, get ready to have more fun reading than a worm has in an apple!

And remember, Girlz Rock!

Shey Kettle.

GIRLZ ROCK!
When We Were Kids

Shey — *Jacqueline*

Shey talked to Jacqueline, another *Girlz Rock!* author.

Shey "Did you go camping when you were little?"

Jacqueline "Yup! We camped by the river but I didn't like it."

Shey "Why not?"

Jacqueline "Well, when I went to sleep, the world's biggest mosquitoes bit me."

Shey "Really, how big were they?"

Jacqueline "They were so big that they carried me a mile away from my tent."

Shey "Oh, no! How did you get back?"

Jacqueline "I woke up!"

GIRLZ ROCK!
What a Laugh!

Q Why didn't the skeleton go camping?

A He had no body to go with!